SWIMMING
OVER CASTLES

DANIELLE HOBBS

To order additional copies of this book, contact:
Xlibris
844-714-8691
www.Xlibris.com
Orders@Xlibris.com

ISBN:	Softcover	978-1-6698-0862-6
	Hardcover	978-1-6698-0864-0
	EBook	978-1-6698-0863-3

Print information available on the last page

Rev. date: 01/28/2022

I hope you enjoy Swimming over Castles! and Remember where ever you go in life, never forget who you are. Remembering who you are and whose you are, will always help you to NEVER swim over your castle.

-Danielle Hobbs

This children's book is a illustrated fantasy about a child that got to go all over the world and never forget who he/she was inside. It is a book speaking in a poetic rhythm and metaphor, capturing the art of self-awareness. The pictures and illustrations are actual images taken while I toured with Cirque Du Soleil, doing the Michael Jackson Immortal World Tour. I hope it inspires children to dream, and grow up to live their biggest dreams.

This book shows that dreams do come true! If you can Dream it! You can Do it!

I dedicate to book to Cirque du Soleil for the opportunity to be a part of such a great project, and go once again around the world.

I dedicate this to Michael Jackson Estate for their support in my global vision of uplifting youth, through Education and Performing Arts, being true to your God Given Gifts.

I also dedicate this book to my Mom and Dad, for always teaching me to believe in myself, and never be afraid of my calling, no matter how unique my path, thank you for supporting me whether I am being a great Performing Artist or in the classroom, always teach others to DREAM, REACH FOR THE STARS!! and most of all TEACH PEOPLE TO LOVE!

Love and Light,

Dream it! Do it! Danigirl!

"Swimming over Castles"

You may swim with friends
in the Mediterranean,
And run in the fields of
forest and trails,

You may fly like an eagle, or a good luck Blue Jay,
But don't swim over your Castle,
Let the tale unveil.

You may peddle your bike over the Great Wall of China,
And ski the highest mountain in France,

You may swim with whales in Hawaii
Then samba over to Brazil's Carnival fast,

You may go through the African Safari,
And the children of Zimbabwe give you a gift.

You can even set sail to Dominican Republic,
To speak Spanish, and see tropical fish.

You may decide to river dance with the Irish,
And bang pipes to the Scottish beat.

You may decide to play double-dutch in Harlem,
While tapping rhythms with your feet.

You may sing an opera in Italy.
And perform a ballet for the queen.
However, do not swim over your castle.
For the there will always be...

Those up to tricks
Those that throw bricks,

Some will say you can't come,
And act like you are no fun.

There will be those that beat around the bush,
And have to make a fuss,

There will be those that say
HUSH!
You are talking too much!

But in the beginning of their stuff,
It always ends with you and your castle.

Don't swim over it, please I say.
For when the court falls asleep,
You still have your castle at bay,

For when the caged bird stops her singing,
And you have to let her fly away, or the lion doesn't roar,
And the dolphin doesn't play,
You still have your castle to soar!

Dolphin Bay
ATLANTIS

And when it is just you and your castle
You will see,

You can dance, flip, hop, and sing,
You can turn, and twist,
You can even clean, the dirty moat,
Hiding the beauty in between.

In your castle you can laugh, cry, scream,
Love, eat, or simply dream.

Now you can swim over it if you like,
But I think you'd like what you find hidden
Inside.

Because it's always going to be you and your castle
For your Castle is You!
GOODNIGHT!

No matter all the places you go in life, never forget who you are; never leave it behind, like show up, for it will always be there when you need it.

ABOUT THE AUTHOR

DANIELLE HOBBS, has always been an story teller! An Impeccable Dancer performer turned singer/songwriter, actress and motivational speaker and author, she graduated with a B.A. in Dance from CSU Long Beach at the age of 19. Hobbs is a triple threat powerhouse performer. Her credits include choreographing on Artists' Beyoncé and Shakira. She also was a premier dancer on the Cirque Du Soleil tour, Michael Jackson Immortal World tour, while flipping upside down and being a MJ Immortal, she got her Masters degree in Education to teach and continue to build her children's book line, "Dream it!

Do it! Danigirl Adventures!" into animated show, with her Youth brand Dream it! Do it! Danigirl!

Adventures she has had as a choreographer include many soulful venues choreographing Beyoncé Knowles-Carter for opening the 2006 World Music Awards, BET and MTV Awards and Grammy performances with Shakira. She has landed lead roles in musical theater as AIDA, in Elton John and Tim Rice's "AIDA," and Brenda, from "Smokey Joe's Café." Danielle has added creating, writing, and producing her first short film and soundtrack on Apple music, "Amethyst Girl Destiny," which she wrote, produced and starred in. Currently, she is an educator Achievement Guide at middle school charter, GARVEY ALLEN STEAM Academy.

Although she is very accomplished, Danielle's highest and best thing to do, is to always inspire and empower the youth where ever she is working to Dream it! Do it! Danigirl! and Live the Life of your Dreams!

I hope you enjoy Swimming over Castles! and Remember where ever you go in life, never forget who you are. Remembering who you are and whose you are, will always help you to NEVER swim over your castle.

Printed in the United States
by Baker & Taylor Publisher Services